Capstone Young Readers
a capstone imprint

Baby Survival Guides
are published by Capstone Young Readers,
a Capstone imprint
1710 Roe Crest Drive
North Mankato, Minnesota 56003
www.mycapstone.com

Cataloging-in-Publication Data is available on
the Library of Congress website.
ISBN: 978-1-62370-611-1 (Paper Over Board)
ISBN: 978-1-62370-634-0 (eBook)

Printed and bound in China
092015   009224S16

A BABY'S GUIDE

TO

Surviving

MOM

by Benjamin Bird

art by Tiago Americo

Hello, baby.

One day, not so long ago,
you were born.

And life gave you a mom.

And life gave Mom everything
she'd ever wanted.

Except instructions!

That's right, baby. Your mom's pretty much just wingin' it.

So in order to survive, you'll need to teach her a few lessons.

First, let Mom know that there's nothing she can't handle.

Well, almost nothing.

**Next, teach Mom
the Dos and Don'ts of babydom.
For example, DO prepare for the worst.**

But DON'T expect the best.

LESSON THREE:

Be sure Mom knows that there is safety in numbers.

Except, of course, Number One
and Number Two.

And always buckle up because, as they say, accidents do happen.

Just not the ones you prepare for.

Finally, teach Mom to live each day (and night!) to the fullest.

Because, as everyone knows, nothing's worse than an empty stomach.

That's it, baby. Soon you'll be in good hands.

**And just remember . . .
you can't survive without Mom.**

**And Mom can't survive
without you.**